THREE EPIC ADVENTURES OF
SUPERTATO

SUE HENDRA & PAUL LINNET

SIMON & SCHUSTER

London New York Sydney Toronto New Delhi

Meet Sue and Paul:

Sue Hendra and **Paul Linnet** have been making books together since 2009 when they came up with *Barry the Fish with Fingers*, and since then they haven't stopped. If you've ever wondered which one does the writing and which does the illustrating, wonder no more . . . they both do both!

I dedicate this book to myself because
everyone else is a NITWIT!
– Evil Pea

SIMON & SCHUSTER
First published in Great Britain in 2023 by Simon & Schuster UK Ltd
1st Floor, 222 Gray's Inn Road, London, WC1X 8HB
Supertato first published in 2014
Supertato: Veggies in the Valley of Doom first published in 2018
Supertato: Carnival Catastro-Pea! first published in 2019
Text and illustrations copyright © 2014, 2018, 2019 Sue Hendra and Paul Linnet
The right of Sue Hendra and Paul Linnet to be identified as the authors and illustrators of this work
has been asserted by them in accordance with the Copyright, Designs and Patents Act, 1988
A CIP catalogue record for this book is available from the British Library upon request
978-1-3985-1778-3 (PB) • 978-1-3985-1779-0 (eBook) • Printed in China • 10 9 8 7 6 5 4 3 2 1

SUPERTATO

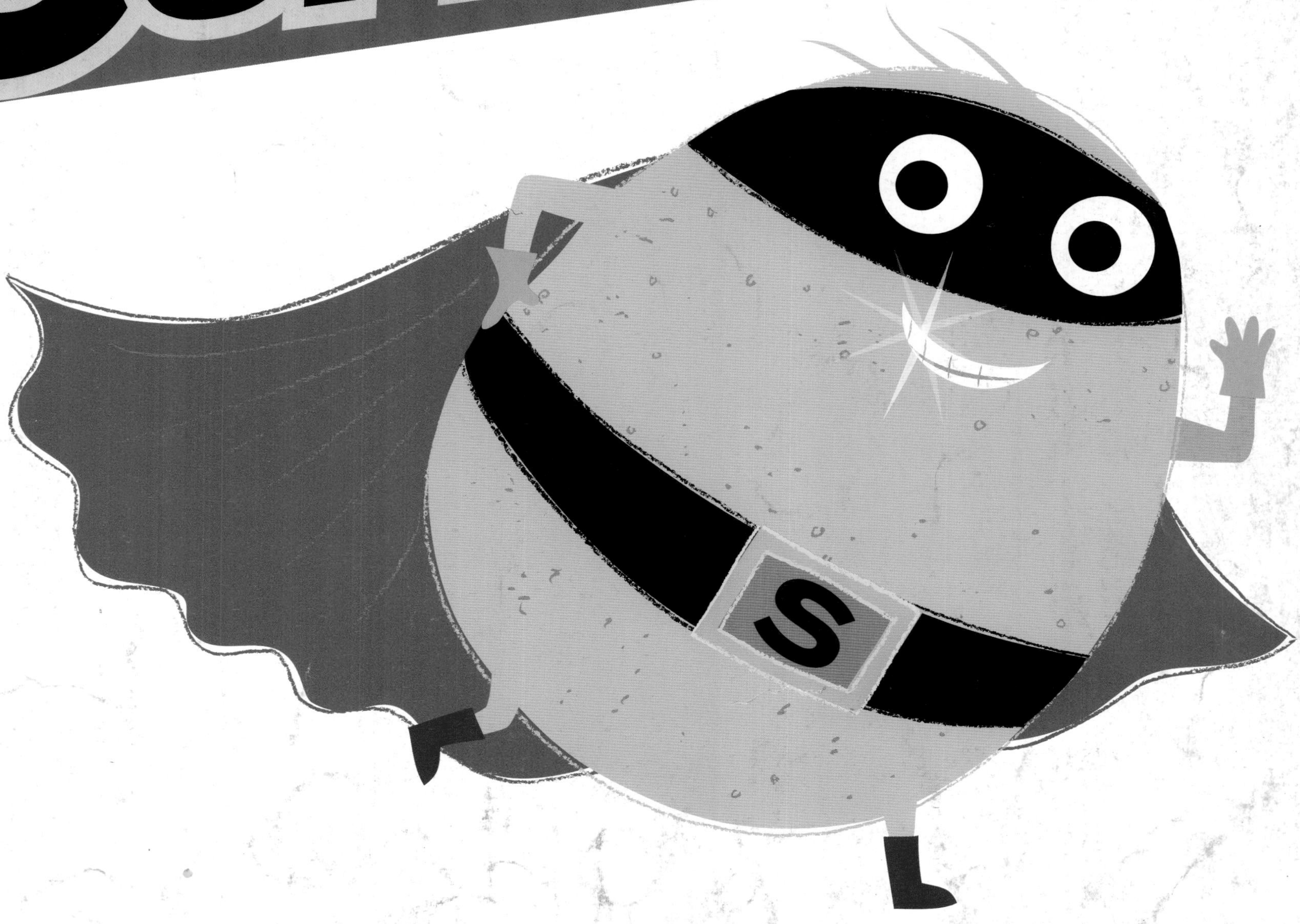

Some vegetables are frozen for a very good reason. Don't believe me? Then keep reading.

It was night-time in the supermarket and all was quiet. But –

crash, bang – something had escaped from the freezer.
Something small and round and green.

Something looking for trouble.
Big trouble.

"Hmmmmpfff!" cried Cucumber.

Who was doing this? And was there anyone who could help these vegetables in distress?

He used his
super speed . . .

He used his
super strength . . .

He used a flannel
and some soapy water.

"I know who's behind this," said Supertato.
"There's a pea on the loose!"
"Oh no – not a pea!" everyone gasped.

"Yes, a pea! But I'm out of the freezer now and I'm never going back! Mwah ha ha ha ha!" And The Evil Pea ran off to commit more terrible crimes.

"Time for a dip, little veggies!"

"That's enough!" shouted Supertato.

He leapt towards the pea, but the pea popped out of his hands and vanished into thin air.

Supertato set out on a super search.
He crept through the cakes . . .

checked the cheese . . .

and snuck up on the beans.
Then something
caught his eye.

"The game's up!" yelled Supertato.

KERPOW!

But the pea bounced out of reach and onto a trolley. Supertato was just about to stop him with his super strength

when the trolley crashed –

and he was thrown down into the icy depths of the freezer.

Was this the end for Supertato?

GASP!

Not quite.

But the pea was off his trolley and lying in wait. "You're finished, Supertato!" he shrieked.

But Supertato summoned up all his strength . . .

and ran for it.

The pea nearly had him at the beans,

and closed in on him at the cheese.

He had him cornered at the cakes.

"So much for Supertato!" screeched the pea.
"You're about to be MASHED POTATO!"

Surely THIS was the end for Supertato?

"Not today, my friend," said Supertato.

"Gotcha!"

"Mmmppfff!" said the pea.

SQUI

"Oh yes," said Supertato. "I set my trap and you fell for it. Or should that be IN it?!" And he grinned a super grin.

Supertato had saved the day.
"Take him away," he said.
And the pea was marched back
to the freezer where he belonged.

"This jelly tastes of pea!"
said Broccoli. And everybody
laughed and cheered.

So, remember, folks . . .

Some vegetables are frozen for
a very good reason. Maybe you'd
better go and check your freezer. Just
in case there's an escapee in your house . . .

SUPERTATO

VEGGIES IN THE VALLEY OF DOOM

It was night-time in the supermarket and the veggies were complaining. "There's nothing to do!" whined Pineapple.

"We could play hide-and-seek?" said Broccoli.
"I'm GREAT at hide-and-seek!"

"What a splendid idea," said Supertato.

So the veggies ran off to hide
and Supertato started to count.

"One . . . two . . . three . . .

. . . four hundred and ninety-eight . . .
four hundred and ninety-nine . . . five hundred!

Ready or not,
here I come!"

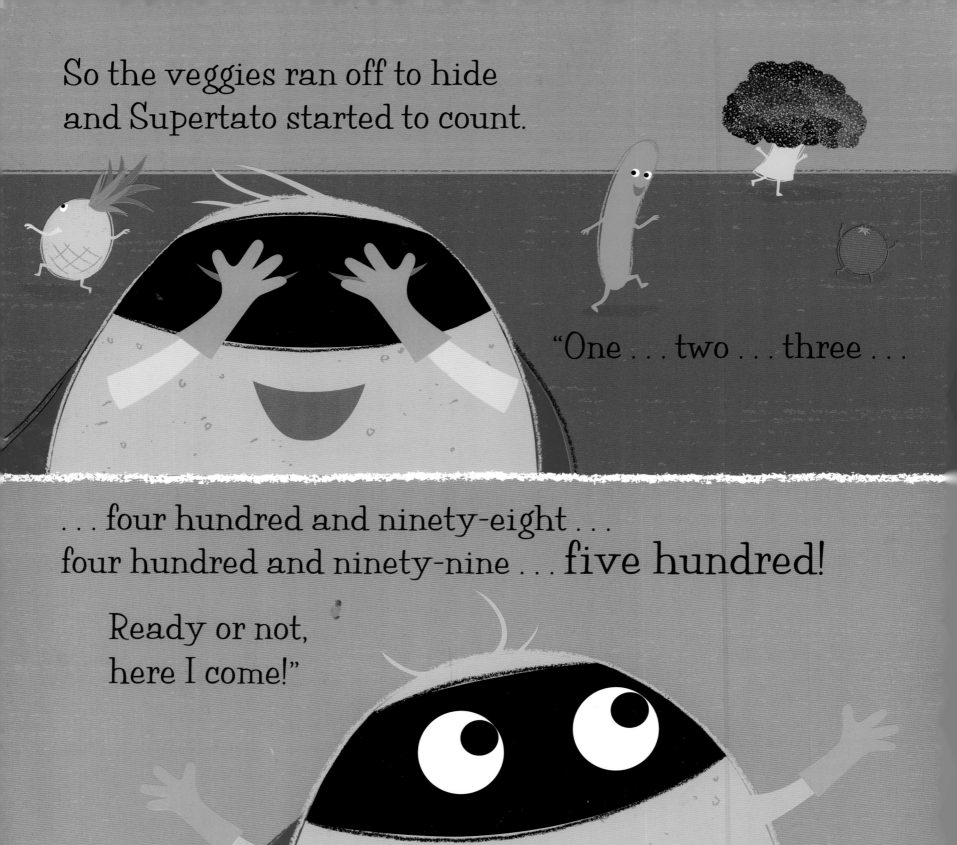

"Hmmm, they must be around here somewhere," thought Supertato.

"Is that you, Tomato?

I can see you, Pineapple!
And you, Cucumber!

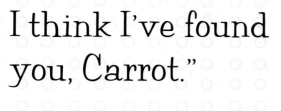

I think I've found you, Carrot."

"You've found ME," said Carrot, "but look what I'VE found . . .

. . . it's a treasure map!"

"You might be right," said Supertato, "and it seems to be leading to the gardening aisle."

As the veggies gathered round, SOMEONE was watching.

"Ooooo, treasure," thought The Evil Pea, from his hiding place.

"Come on, let's go!" shouted the veggies.

"Not so fast," said Supertato. "First we're going to need some supplies."

And he rounded up some water, biscuits, rope and, of course, a pair of oven gloves.

Eh?

But the entrance to the gardening aisle was a wall of plants.

"We'll never get through that!" said Carrot.

"Ah," said Supertato, "that's what the water's for . . ." and with that, he poured it into the pots.

Slurp, slurp, slurp went the plants and up they sprang, clearing the way ahead.

"Thanks, Supertato, we were gasping!"
"Wow," said Tomato. "I didn't know plants could talk!"

"Come on everyone, this way," said Carrot. "The map says we need to go through the Valley of Doom."

"Hmmm . . . why is it called the Valley of Doom?" wondered Pineapple . . .

. . . but he didn't wonder for long.

"Quick, Pineapple, it's crunch time," shouted Supertato. "Throw me the biscuits!"

Luckily, the biscuits did the trick and Supertato and the veggies were soon out of danger. PHEW!

But now they'd reached a dead end.
"This must be Cactus Canyon," said Carrot.

"We'll get prickled to pieces!" cried Tomato.
"How will we ever get through?"

"With oven gloves, of course!" said Supertato,
and soon they were back on their way.

It was a long trek through the desert.
"I can't go on," said Tomato.
"Yes, you can," said Supertato.
"Together we're all going to make it."

After hours of walking they were finally
out of the desert.

"I can see a treasure chest!" shouted Carrot.
"We're almost there!"

But Supertato and the veggies
were so excited, they didn't see . . .

. . . the quicksand!

"Help! Help!" they yelled. "We're sinking fast!"

"*Mwah ha ha ha ha!*" shrieked The Evil Pea.
"You ARE in a sticky situation!"

"Oh dear," said one cactus to another,
"is this the end for Supertato and the veggies?"

Maybe it was. With Supertato
in the quicksand, who could help
these veggies in distress?

"Well, don't look at me!"
shouted the pea.
"The treasure's mine, ALL mine!"

"Please, please help us, Pea," called the veggies.
"Before it's too late . . ."

"OH, ALL RIGHT," snapped the pea.
"IF I MUST."

Supertato threw the rope and the pea pulled them to safety.

"You saved us!" squealed the veggies.

"You're a hero!"

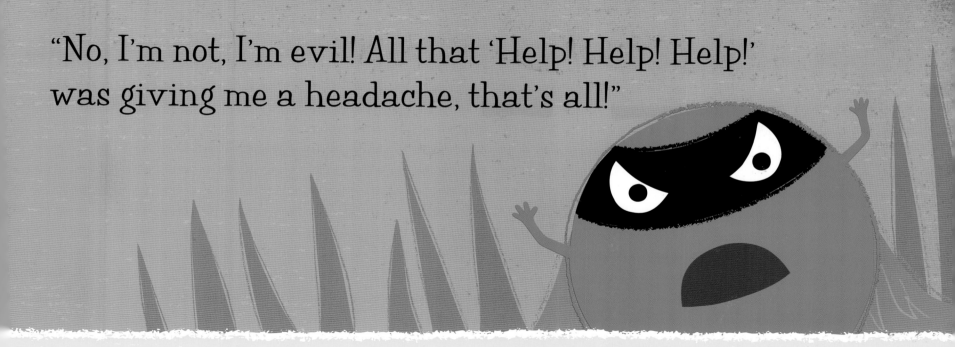

"No, I'm not, I'm evil! All that 'Help! Help! Help!' was giving me a headache, that's all!"

Supertato smiled. The moment had come.
Everyone crowded around the treasure chest –
it was time to see what was inside . . .

"**SURPRISE!!!!!**" yelled Broccoli,
popping out of the treasure chest.
"I told you I was GREAT
at hide-and-seek!"

Supertato and the gang started
the long walk home.

"I didn't have you down as one of
the good guys, Pea," said Supertato,
"but maybe I was wrong . . ."

"*Mwah ha ha ha ha!* Whatever you say, Supertato," sniggered the pea.

It was night-time in the supermarket
and our fearless crime-fighting hero
was having to gather ALL his strength . . .

. . . to tie up some party balloons!

The veggies had been busy preparing
for the Supermarket Carnival for months.

"There you go, Carrot. This place is looking amazing!

How's the banner going, Cucumber?"

"I'm just off to get some more paint, Supertato."

"Thanks to all your hard work," said Supertato, "this carnival is going to be a wonderful celebration of colour and fun!"

But **someone** had other ideas. "That's what **you** think," sniggered The Evil Pea from his hiding place.

BAD SCIENCE

"I **hate** colour and I **hate** fun. Let's see those nitwits try and celebrate when I unleash this!"

"EVERYONE!" shouted Supertato.
"Can I have your attention, please!
It's the day we've all been waiting for.
I now declare this carnival . . ."

" . . . RUINED!" screeched the pea as he leapt onto the stage. "Behold my new invention – the Colour-Suck-A-Tron-5000.

It's going to suck the colour out of everything!

"And who wants to be next? How about you 'Red' Chilli? Or should I just call you Chilli from now on?

No more green for you, Green Bean!

Goodbye Blueberry, hello Greyberry!" cackled the pea.

He was out of control. And the veggies knew it.

"SAVE ME!" cried the greyberry.

"SAVE US ALL!"
But who could help these veggies in distress?

There could be only one . . .

"What's he done to us, Supertato?"
"I don't know, Tomato."
"I'm not Tomato, I'm Orange!"
said Orange.

The supermarket was a sad sight – the balloons
and banners, the flags and costumes,
everything was ruined.
"Why did you do it, Pea?"

"Well, Supertato, I'm glad you asked," hissed the pea. "It's not easy being mean . . . but **someone's** got to do it!

Mwah ha ha ha ha!"

And with that, off he sped to wreak more havoc.

"Hmmm, looks like the end for the carnival," said one pineapple to the other . . .

"Hang on a minute, look who's just walked in!"

It was Cucumber.
"I've found the paint, Supertato!"
But then she froze. "What's happened here?"

"THERE YOU ARE, CUCUMBER!" said Supertato.
"The pea stole all of our colours but you may just
have given me a great idea . . ."

"Blueberries, I'm going to need your help.

Cucumber, I'm going to need your green paint."

There wasn't a moment to lose.

So Cucumber painted the blueberries,

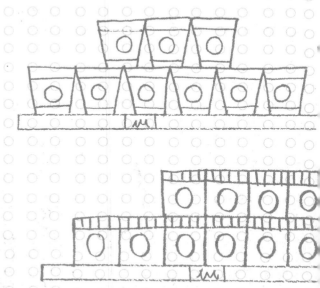

which wasn't easy.

Carrot gave them some masks,

Tomato gave them some acting lessons

and Supertato gave them a speech.
"Find that pea, pretend to be his evil pea
friends and let's get our carnival back!"

The Evil Pea didn't suspect a thing.

"About time!
This is really heavy,"
spat the pea as he handed
them the Suck-a-Tron.

"Well, go on then, point it at something!"

So they did.

And once the pea was in position, it was time to flick the switch from colour-sucker to colour-blaster.

It wasn't long before . . .

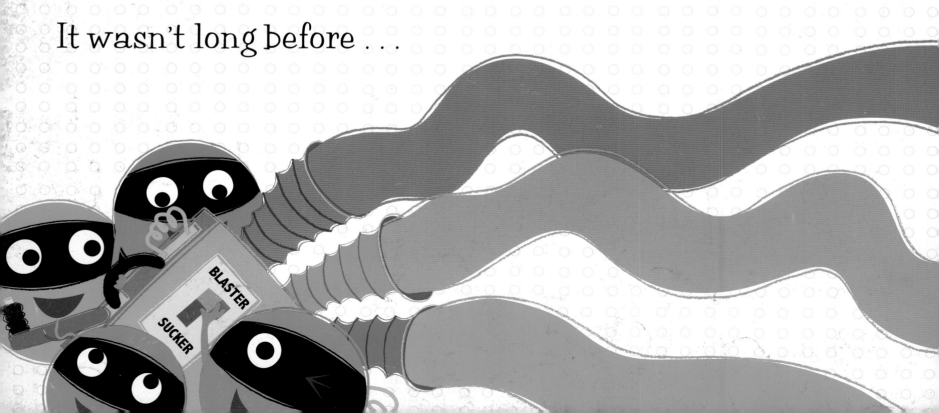

Tomato was red again,

Orange was orange again

and Supertato was that potatoey-colour-that-doesn't-have-a-name again.

Everything was as it should be, and it was time . . .

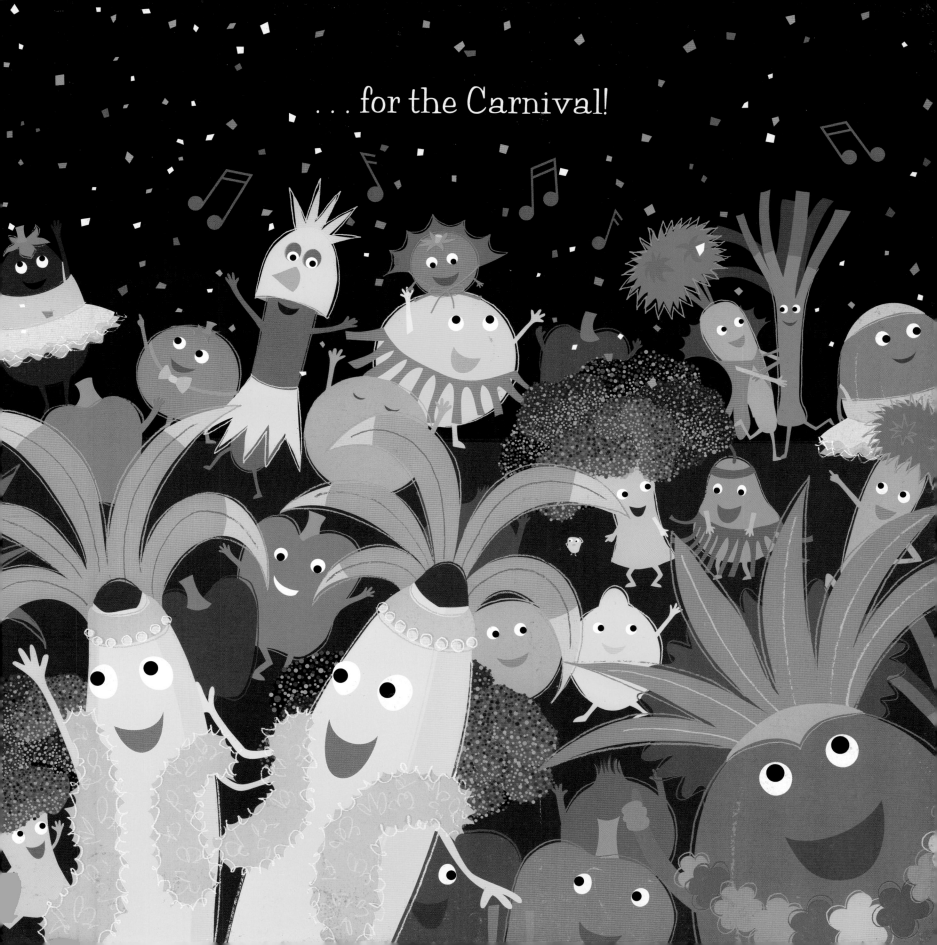

. . . for the Carnival!

"There you are, Blueberries!
Goodness me, you have been busy.
That's the most colourful thing I've ever seen!
What a shame that Evil Pea isn't here to see it.

I wonder where he could be . . . ?"

If you like

SUPERTATO

you'll love these other

adventures from

SUE HENDRA & PAUL LINNET

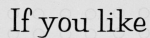

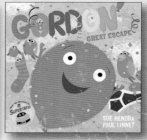

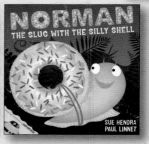